SHH! THE WHALE IS SMILING

GREEN TIGER PRESS

Published by Simon & Schuster · New York

London · Toronto · Sydney · Tokyo · Singapore

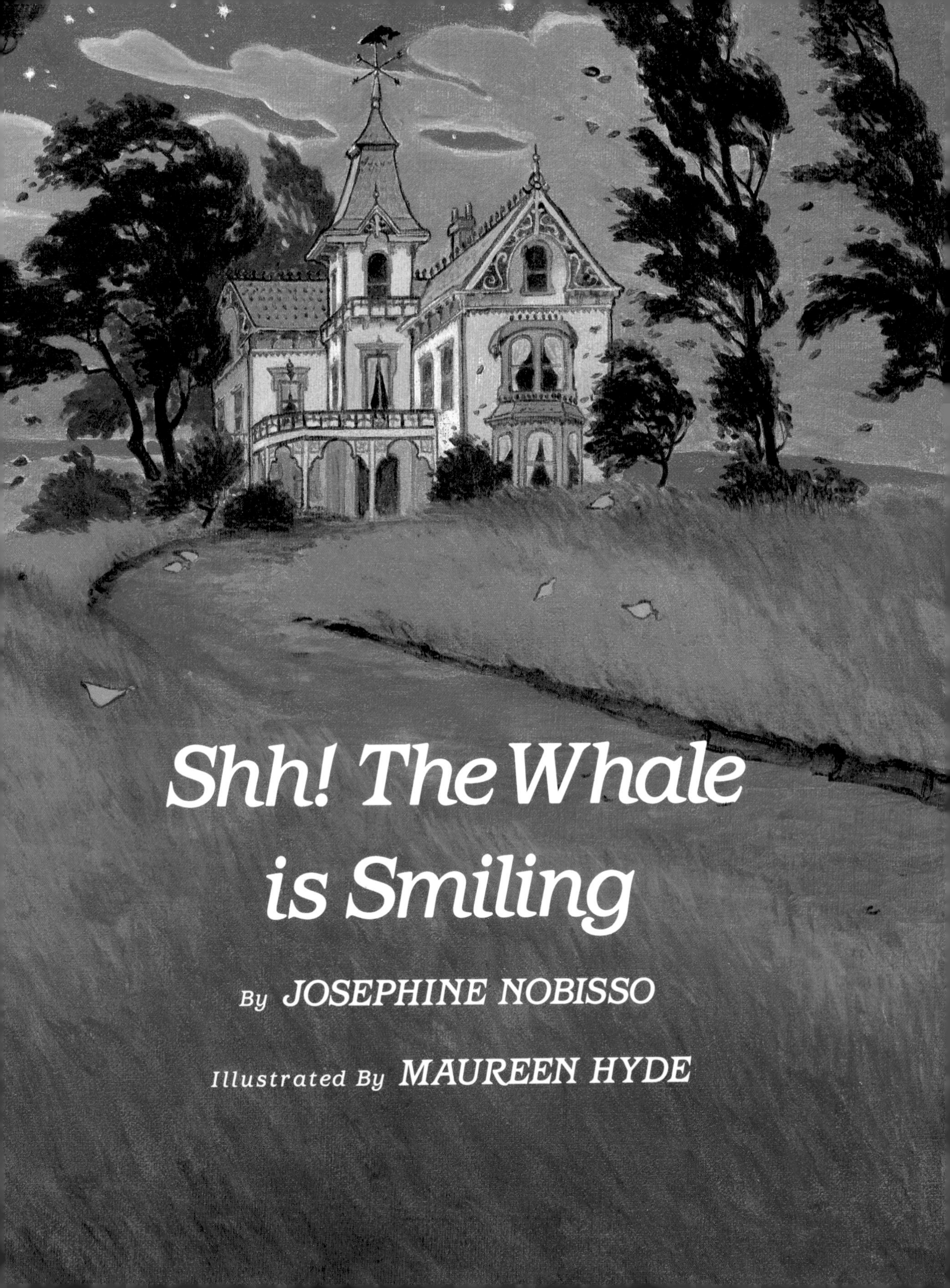
Shh! The Whale is Smiling
By JOSEPHINE NOBISSO
Illustrated By MAUREEN HYDE

For my sister
Suzy (Mary Susan)
and my brother-in-law,
Salvatore Golfo,
who have always
believed

—J.N.

For Leita and Theo,
and in loving memory
of my mother

—M.H.

GREEN TIGER PRESS
Simon & Schuster Building
Rockefeller Center
1230 Avenue of the Americas
New York, New York, 10020

GREEN TIGER PRESS is an imprint of
Simon & Schuster
Designed by Joy Chu
Manufactured in Hong Kong
10 9 8 7 6 5 4 3 2 1

Library of Congress Cataloging-in-Publication Data
Nobisso, Josephine.
Shh!—the whale is smiling / by Josephine Nobisso ;
illustrated by Maureen Hyde.
p. cm.
Summary: A bedtime tale in the dark evokes the wonder
of the whale as it swims, smiles, and sings.
[1. Whales—Fiction. 2. Bedtime—Fiction. 3. Night—Fiction.]
I. Hyde, Maureen, ill. II. Title.
PZ7.N6645Sh 1992
[E]—dc20 91-21521 CIP AC
ISBN 0-671-74908-0

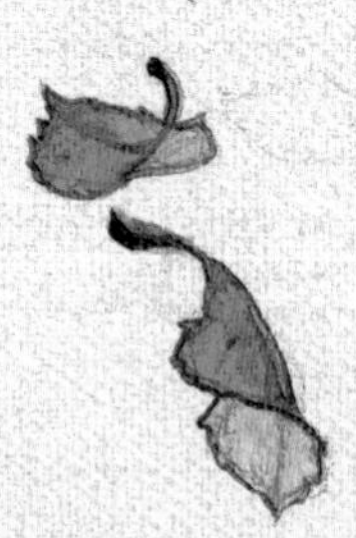

Shh! The wind is swirling.

And I am here beside you

In the dark–

In the soft, warm cozy darkness

Of the night.

Shhh! The bed is swaying.
It's tipping, dipping, spinning,
Like a tired top
Humming through
The thick of night.

Shhh! The sea is rocking.
We are swimming
Near a whale,
Gentle as a butterfly,
Bigger than a bus.

Shh! The whale is smiling.
His loving eye is glistening
As he watches us and guides us
Through the floating, flying freedom
Of the deep.

Shh! We are rolling.

He takes us whirling,

Gently twirling

While swelling bubbles burst

Like happiness in the heart.

Shh! The whale is singing.
He hums a booming mystery
That sways us
In a rumbling, shivering hammock
Made of waves.

Shh! We are rolling.

Shh! The whale is singing.

Shh! The whale is smiling.

Shh! The sea is rocking.

Shh! The bed is swaying.

Shh! The wind is swirling.

Shh! Shh!

And I am here beside you

In the dark—

In the soft, warm cozy darkness

Of this night.

Shhhh!